The Movie Storybook

Storybook adaptation by
Cathy East Dubowski

Illustrated by Renzo Barto

Based on characters created by
Jean and Laurent de Brunhoff

Random House 🏠 New York

Based on BABAR—THE MOVIE

Screenplay by Peter Sauder, J.D. Smith,
John de Klein, and Raymond Jafelice

Library of Congress Cataloging-in-Publication Data:
Dubowski, Cathy East. Babar, the movie storybook : based on Babar—the movie / by Cathy East Dubowski ; illustrated by Renzo Barto.
p. cm. "Based on the screenplay written by Peter Sauder...[et al.]"—T.p. verso. SUMMARY: After the annual Victory Day celebration, King Babar tells his children about his early days as king and how the first Victory Day came to be. ISBN: 0-394-84528-5 [1. Elephants—Fiction]
I. Barto, Renzo, ill. II. Babar—the movie. III. Title. PZ7.D8544Bab 1989 [E]—dc20 89-33398

Manufactured in the United States of America 1 2 3 4 5 6 7 8 9 10

Arthur
Babar's cousin

Young Babar
Boy king of the Elephants

Young Celeste
Babar's cousin

Croc
A grateful crocodile

Zephir
Babar's monkey friend from the jungle

The Old Lady
Babar's friend from the city

Rataxes
Evil king of the Rhinos

Cornelius
Adviser to King Babar

The sun was just rising over the castle of King Babar. But already people were gathering along the main avenue of the city.

Schools and offices were closed. Families had the whole day to spend together. And all the elephants were dressed up in their most festive clothes.

For it was Victory Day, the elephants' favorite holiday.

Suddenly drums and trumpets sounded through the crisp morning air—

The Victory Day Parade was coming!

The elephants pressed closer to the curb as the royal marching band stomped by, playing the elephant anthem. Clowns somersaulted in and out of the crowd. Flags and banners colored the sky, and flower girls showered the street with exotic blossoms.

A small elephant sitting high on her father's shoulders pulled excitedly on his big ears and pointed in the distance. "Look!" she cried. "A giant!"

High in the sky a fierce elephant towered above the crowd. The children screamed...just as they did every year. And then their screams dissolved, as always, into delighted giggles. For they knew it wasn't a *real* giant—it was only a giant balloon! On the street below, the strongest elephants strained to hold the ropes that kept the bobbing giant from sailing off into the sky.

In a small basket hanging from the balloon, King Babar's cousin Arthur raised a huge horn to his lips. *Brraaappp!* went the horn, and the giant elephant seemed to trumpet a rousing call to arms.

Then someone shouted, "Here comes the royal coach!" and everyone began to cheer, for all the elephants loved and admired their royal family. King Babar and Queen Celeste waved to their loyal friends. Their children—Pom, Flora, Alexander, and Isabelle—tossed trunkfuls of peanuts to the children in the crowd.

As the parade meandered through the town, King Babar squeezed Queen Celeste's hand. "How lucky we are indeed," he said, "to live in a kingdom that is peaceful and free...."

The Victory Day celebration lasted far into the night as fireworks sparkled the evening sky. Yet all too soon it was bedtime. Mothers and fathers throughout the kingdom began to tuck their children in for the night.

But just like most of those young elephants, the royal children were still far too excited to sleep.

"Can we have another parade tomorrow?" asked Isabelle, the youngest, as King Babar tucked the bedcovers up under her chin.

"I'm afraid you'll have to wait till next year," her father answered. "Victory Day comes only once a year."

"Why is it called Victory Day?" asked Isabelle.

"Well," said Babar, "that's a long story..."

"Good!" said Isabelle.

And all the children spoke at once, begging to hear the tale.

"All right, all right!" King Babar said, laughing, for he loved to tell stories as much as the children loved to hear them. The young elephants tumbled into Isabelle's bed, shushing and poking one another to settle down.

"The story of Victory Day began a long time ago," Babar said, "when I was just a boy." And as he wove his vivid tale, each child imagined what it must have been like to be a young king of the elephants many, many years ago....

It was young Babar's first day as king. Oh, how he had dreamed of this day! What adventures he would have! What great things he would do! What important decisions he would have to make!

Babar was excited—nervous, too—but fortunately his good friend the Old Lady was there with him. His advisers Cornelius, Pompadour, and Troubadour had a lot of experience to share with him. And of course his cousin Arthur was by his side as well.

"Now, then," said Cornelius, loudly clearing his throat. "What monumental problem must we look at today?"

Troubadour wrote down a long message on a fancy piece of royal paper. He walked formally across the room and, with a courtly bow, placed it in Pompadour's hand.

Pompadour read the message. "Ah, yes. Most urgent indeed!"

At last! thought Babar. An important decision to make!

"Today," Pompadour announced, "we must decide upon a new parade mascot."

Oh, no! thought Babar as the Royal Mascot Committee hurried into the room and set up their briefcases and easels and charts.

The first committee member stepped forward. "We tried to pick a mascot that would symbolize all the things we most admire," he said, pointing to his charts and flipping pictures. "One that would have the courage of a lion, the wisdom of an owl, the serenity of a giraffe, the diligence of a beaver, and the dignity of a zebra."

"But," said another committee member, "we couldn't decide on just one." She went to her model and dramatically pulled off the cover. The new mascot looked like all those other animals mixed up into one! "So we used them all. What do you think, Your Majesty?"

Cornelius, Troubadour, and Pompadour studied it seriously. Arthur hooted with laughter.

"It looks rather...complicated," Babar said. Then he asked, "Why don't we just use an *elephant* as our mascot?"

At that everyone began talking at once. Babar tried to hide a yawn. Being king was not quite as exciting as he had imagined it would be.

Just then voices at the door to the throne room captured Babar's attention. His friend Celeste was struggling to get past the royal guards. At last she broke through and ran to Babar. She was out of breath and could hardly speak. "Babar—you must send your army—at once..."

"Celeste!" cried Arthur. "What are you doing here? I thought you went with Mama to visit Grandpa out in the country!"

"I did," she said. "But the rhinos and their leader, Rataxes, are on a rampage throughout the countryside. They're attacking villages and kidnapping elephants. And Grandfather's village could be next! I ran all the way back to get help!"

"Don't worry," Babar said. "I'll order the army to leave at once. And I'll even lead it myself."

"Thank you, Babar," Celeste said with a warm smile. "I knew I could count on you."

Then she hurried off to tell the villagers that help was on the way.

But as the sun went down over the castle that night, Babar's advisers were still talking and debating and planning.

"We shouldn't rush into this," insisted Cornelius.

"You're right," Pompadour agreed. "We must surely look at all the facts before we act."

"Could be just a rumor, you know," added Cornelius.

Frustrated, Babar left the castle and followed a familiar road to a cottage that sat by a gentle brook. It was the home of his friend the Old Lady. He knew he could always talk to her.

"Why does everything have to take so long!" he asked after going inside. "Cornelius says it will take at least three days to get our army ready. That may be too late. The rhinos could be attacking Celeste's village right now!"

The Old Lady rocked gently back and forth, thinking as she worked a few stitches in her knitting. After a quiet moment, she asked: "What do *you* think you should do?"

Babar bit his lip; he wasn't sure.

The Old Lady kept knitting, but added softly, "You must do what you *feel* is right."

Babar thought hard for a moment. Then he smiled. "You're right," he said. "I know what I have to do.... Thanks." He hugged his dear friend, then hurried back to the castle.

The Old Lady stood by the window and watched him go. "Be careful, Babar," she murmured.

"It has to work," said Babar. "While you stay here and pretend to be me, I can slip out and help Celeste."

"You can't stop the rhinos all by yourself!" said Arthur.

But Babar was already climbing down the rope ladder he had hung out the window. "Maybe I can't," he said. "But I have to try." Then he slipped out of sight into the night.

Soon the young elephant king was in his room. He had changed out of his royal clothes and now stood before a full-length mirror with his cousin Arthur—who just happened to look a lot like Babar. And Arthur was wearing the king's crown.

Nervously Arthur eyed his image in the mirror. "Are you sure this is going to work?"

The crescent moon gave off little light as Babar struggled to find his way through the dark jungle. Strange rustling noises followed him, and the yellow eyes of night animals gleamed through the darkness.

At last, up ahead, a bright light broke the black night.

"That must be Celeste's village!" Babar thought, relieved. But his happiness turned to fear when he saw that the brightness came not from evening torchlight—but from the flames of burning huts.

Babar ran to the center of the village. Cruel-eyed rhinos stomped through the noise and confusion, setting fire to the elephants' straw huts. Pottery lay smashed on the ground.

Big baskets of precious food had been spilled into the dirt.
Soldiers yanked screaming babies from their parents' arms while
other rhinos chained up their parents.

Babar looked everywhere for Celeste. When at last he found
her, she was being held—kicking and screaming—by a huge
rhino soldier. Yards away her mother struggled to escape a
tangle of ropes.

"Run, Celeste! Save yourself!" cried her mother as the rhinos
bound her in chains and began to drag her away.

Bravely Babar charged the huge rhinos, but there were just too
many for a small elephant to fight alone. Then someone struck
him on the head, and everything went black.

When Babar woke up,
it was morning. The rhinos
were gone. Where once a
beautiful elephant village had
stood, only smoldering ashes
remained.

The sound of someone
calling brought Babar to his
feet. "Help! Help! Somebody
get me out of here!"

It was Celeste—calling from
the bottom of the village well!

"That soldier threw me
down here so I couldn't
follow my mother!" she called
to Babar as he lowered a
rope into the well for her to
climb up.

When Celeste reached the
top, she looked around
with surprise. "Babar, what
happened? I thought you were
bringing your army."

Babar stared at the ground.
"I'm afraid they won't be
ready for a few more days...."

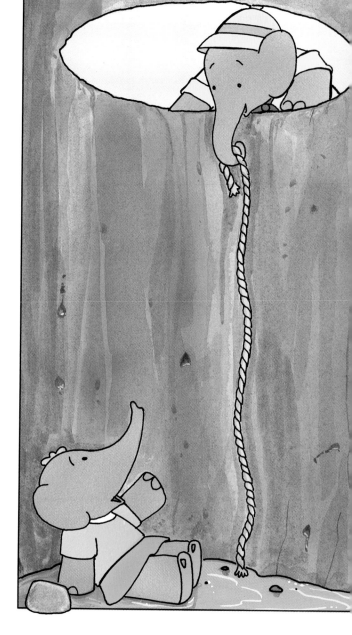

"A few more days!" shouted Celeste. "That will be too late—
the rhino army will be miles away by then." Tears began to fill
her eyes, but she angrily wiped them away with her trunk.
Then, without a word, she turned and ran toward the jungle to
find her mother.

"Wait!" Babar shouted.

Celeste paused at the edge of the clearing.

"This time I'm coming with you," Babar said. "We'll find your
mother together."

Babar and Celeste hiked for miles through thick jungle. They climbed rocky riverbanks and slid down muddy hills. Once they had to cross a deep gorge on a rickety rope bridge. Finally they sat down by a river to rest.

"This is hopeless!" said Celeste. "I think we're lost!"

"Don't worry," said Babar. "We'll find our way, I'm sure of it." But he sounded far more certain than he felt.

Sighing, Babar took off his hat and fanned his brow. Suddenly the hat was snatched from his trunk. He looked at Celeste. She looked at him. And then they both looked up into the canopy of dark leaves above them.

The branches shook with monkey laughter.

"Who are you?" asked the monkey who held Babar's hat.

"This is my friend Celeste," said Babar. With a deep bow he added, "And I am Babar, King of the Elephants."

"Didya hear that, fellas?" cried the monkey to his friends. "We're in the presence of royalty!" With a comical bow, he added, "I'm Zephir the monkey—at your service, O noble one!"

To the delight of his buddies, Zephir began to swing from branch to branch, showing off for his new audience. But then he swung out on a branch that broke, and he tumbled with a great splash into the river.

A hungry crocodile waiting below almost ate him! But Babar quickly jammed a tree branch into the crocodile's mouth so he couldn't close his jaws.

Zephir was quite impressed. "Thanks, King. Now I owe you one," he said. "You do something for me, I do something for you. That's the law of the jungle. Anything—you name it!"

"All right," said Babar. "Help us find Rataxes, king of the rhinos."

With a sudden *swoosh* all the monkeys disappeared into the trees.

"Nobody *wants* to find Rataxes," whispered Zephir. "You want my advice? Turn around and go home!"

"But they've captured my mother!" cried Celeste.

"And we're going to rescue her," said Babar.

"Oh yeah?" said Zephir. "And who's going to rescue you?"

But when he saw how determined the two young elephants were, he told them how to find Rataxes' fortress.

"Good luck, pal!" shouted Zephir as he and his monkey friends swung off through the trees. "Believe me, you'll need it!"

Babar and Celeste turned to leave. But Babar saw the crocodile, thrashing in the river, still struggling with the tree branch stuck between his jaws.

"We can't just leave him like that," said Babar. He waded into the river and gently pulled the branch from the crocodile's mouth.

Celeste looked on with horror, certain that the crocodile would eat her friend in one big bite.

But the crocodile, whose name was Croc, was as surprised as Celeste by Babar's kindness. "Thanks for helping me," said Croc. "Now I owe you one. That's the law of the jungle." With a splash of his great tail, he dived back out into the river, where all his crocodile friends were waiting and watching.

"Now," Babar said to Celeste, "let's go find your mom."

Following Zephir's expert directions, Babar and Celeste soon found the great fortress of Rataxes. With horror, they saw many elephants working there as slaves. Rhino soldiers cracked their whips and shouted at the elephants, forcing them to haul huge stones to build the fortress even larger.

Babar and Celeste waited. When the time was right, they hid in the back of a supply wagon that soon rumbled inside the main gate. Then they slipped out and sneaked into the castle. They were not yet sure what they were going to do, but they knew they must not give up until they had freed all the elephants.

"Look!" whispered Celeste. They were on a ledge high above the throne room, and they could see Rataxes on his throne, bragging to his soldiers about how big and bad he was. Celeste inched forward, then gasped as a loose rock tumbled from the ledge. It hit a soldier square on the head, and he slumped to the ground.

Before the two elephants could hide, Rataxes looked up and saw them. "Guards!" he shouted. "Get them—now!"

Babar and Celeste did their best to escape. But no matter which way they turned, no matter which hall they ran down or which door they tried, they always came face to face with the guards.

Until at last they were surrounded.

Babar and Celeste huddled together in darkness as the prison door clanged shut, locking them both in the dark cell. Rataxes snickered at them through the bars.

Babar stood up to bravely face his enemy. "I am Babar, King of the Elephants, and I demand that you release all of the elephants immediately!"

Rataxes roared with laughter. "Well, you'll have to excuse me, Your Majesty," he answered sarcastically. "BECAUSE I'M OFF TO CRUSH YOUR PUNY LITTLE KINGDOM TO A PULP!" Still laughing, he hurried off to gather his army for battle.

Later, as the prison guard lay snoring, an unexpected visitor sneaked into the dungeon. Zephir the monkey grinned at his two elephant friends as he stole the keys from the guard and unlocked the cells. At last they were all free again!

"I told you I owed you one," Zephir said.

"Now what are we going to do?" moaned Celeste.

A familiar tender voice called out to her from the next cell: "Celeste—is that you?"

Celeste ran to the edge of her cell. "Mama!" she cried. Tears of happiness streamed down her face as she stretched her trunk toward her mother. They were in prison, but at least they were together again.

"We'll get out of here somehow," Babar said as he watched their reunion. "I promise you that!"

Quickly they freed the other elephants. By then Rataxes had already left with most of the soldiers, so it was easy to overcome the few remaining guards.

"Thank you, King Babar," Celeste's mother said. "How can we ever repay you?"

Babar thought quickly. "Go to the other villages in the countryside and gather all the elephants," he said. "Then come to the palace as fast as you can. I've got to try to warn the palace before Rataxes gets there."

"I'm coming with you!" said Celeste.

"And me too," said Zephir, popping up under Babar's hat.

The sun burned hot as the three friends hurried through the thick jungle. Once again they had to use the rope bridge to cross the gorge. But this time the worn ropes broke—and they tumbled into the river below! Clinging together for dear life, they plunged over the roaring rapids.

But then they found themselves rising gently above the water.

"Guess who?" came a voice beneath Babar. The crocodile he had helped had come to their rescue.

"Like I said, I owe you one!" he said. Celeste and Zephir surfaced on the backs of his friends.

Then Babar explained that they were racing to reach the castle before Rataxes attacked.

"It's about time someone taught those rotten rhino troublemakers to keep their horns out of other people's business!" said Croc. "You can count on me, Babar—and every crocodile in the jungle!"

The crocodiles carried them safely and quickly downriver. But by the time they arrived at the castle, it was dark. Several campfires burned not far from the gates—Rataxes and his army were already there.

"We'll never get past all those soldiers," whispered Celeste.

"I've got an idea," said Babar. "Come on." The three sneaked under a tent flap. When they came out, they were standing one on top of the other, wearing an army cloak, hoping to pass as a rhino soldier in the dark night.

But the disguise did not work for long. Rataxes spotted them and shouted at his soldiers to catch them.

Babar spotted a catapult. "Quick—get in!" he told his friends.
Then he picked up an ax lying next to it.

"What does this thing do?" asked Celeste.

"You'll see," said Babar.

Babar struck the rope with the ax—and the catapult tossed
them into the air, up, up, and over the castle walls....

They splashed down into the city's public fountain.

"What is the meaning of this!" sputtered a dripping
Cornelius. He had just been walking by with Troubadour,
Pompadour, the Old Lady, and Arthur—who was still wearing
Babar's crown.

"Swimming in public fountains is strictly forbidden!" said
Pompadour.

"Babar—you're back!" cried Arthur.

"Babar?" cried Cornelius, looking back and forth between the two cousins. Now he wasn't sure who was king. "What's going on here?"

"Allow me, Arthur," said the Old Lady. She removed the crown from Arthur's head and placed it on Babar's. Then Babar explained everything.

"But now there's no more time for talk," said Babar. "It's time for action."

Babar jumped up on the back of a wagon. "Citizens of Elephantland," he said. "Our city has been free for as long as anyone can remember. The rhinos want to make us their slaves. They have us outnumbered, but I have a plan that I think will outsmart them. Are you with me?"

"Yes!" they all shouted.

"Then listen closely," said King Babar. "Here's what we're going to do...."

Everyone was busy as the sun rose over the land of the elephants. Some sewed together big gray flannel blankets. Others filled balloons. The royal drummers lined up with their instruments. Celeste and Zephir gathered all the fireworks they could find.

Soon everything was ready. King Babar stepped outside the gates, with Cornelius and Pompadour at his side.

"What is your answer?" bellowed Rataxes. "Do you surrender—or do we destroy you?"

Babar stared bravely into Rataxes' eyes. "Either take your army and leave—now—or suffer the consequences."

"You dare to threaten me?" cried Rataxes. "I'll show you!" Angrily shouting at the top of his lungs, he ordered his army to attack.

But just then the ground began to tremble. The rhinos stopped in their tracks, frightened.

And then a giant elephant rose above the castle gates as fireworks exploded in the sky.

Rataxes' soldiers nearly trampled one another as they tried to run away. But their escape was blocked by a whole herd of angry elephants, with Celeste's mother leading the way.

So the terrified rhinos ran the only other way they could—into the river. Another surprise awaited them there.

"Guess who?" said Croc, splashing up out of the water. Then he and his crocodile friends chased the rhinos downriver.

The elephants were overjoyed! Rataxes and his powerful army had been fooled by their quick-thinking young king—and by a giant elephant made out of blanket-covered balloons!

To celebrate, the elephants held a parade that very day. And King Babar proclaimed Victory Day a national holiday, so that every year they could once again celebrate their freedom.

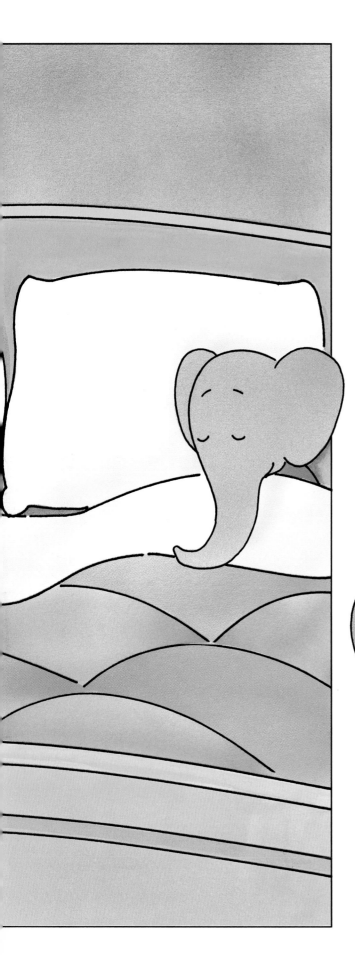

Now, years later, the grown King Babar was telling the story to his children.

"And that is why we celebrate Victory Day with a big parade," he said. "Did you like the story?"

But no one answered, for Isabelle, Pom, Flora, and Alexander had all fallen fast asleep.

Babar smiled and kissed each sleeping child good night.

"Seems like only yester-day..." he said as he turned out the light.